Pig's curly wurly tail

This book belongs to…

....

Pig's curly wurly tail

Written by Jillian Harker
Illustrated by Simon Abbott

Bright ☆ Sparks

The animals at Goosefeather Farm were worried. Cockerel stood on the gatepost, looking at Pig's sty.

"What on earth's the matter with Pig?" he asked.

"I don't know," said Cat, scratching her head. "He's been like that for days."

"Then it's time someone spoke to him," announced Cow. "And I'm the one to do it."

She hurried across the farmyard, clanging her large bell!

Pig was slumped in his sty,
feeling sorry for himself.

He was lying with his chin on his feet, staring up at the sky. Pig was very fed up and he didn't feel like moving. He didn't even lift his head at the sound of Cow's bell.

"Good morning, Pig," said Cow. "If you don't mind me mentioning it, you don't look very happy. Is anything wrong?"

"Tut!" muttered Pig. "It's all right for you!"

"Is it?" asked Cow, confused.

"You've got a tail that does something useful," Pig continued. "Not like mine!"

"Oh," said Cow, "if that's all that's bothering you, it's easy.

Just give your tail a good flick – like this."

She slapped her tail across her back and flicked off a fly that was sunbathing there.

Pig got to his feet, very slowly, and turned to look at his tail.

He thought very hard.

"Flick, tail, flick," he told his tail. But it just sat there, curled round in a tight little knot.

"You see! You see!" wailed Pig.
"I told you it was useless!"

"Oh dear," thought Cow, as she
tiptoed quietly away. "Just wait
until the others hear about this."

"Don't worry," said Goose, when she heard Cow's story. "I'll sort this out," and she waddled across to Pig's sty.

"Cheer up, Pig," she called. "Of course you can't flick your tail like Cow. Her tail is *much* longer than yours."

"That's all very well for you," sniffed Pig. "You've got a short tail, too, but you can waggle it about, can't you?"

"Well, yes," said Goose, "but I'm sure you could too, with a bit of practice. Here, let me show you."

Goose took hold of Pig's tail and waggled it from side to side.

"Nothing to it," she said. "Now you have a go." And she let go of Pig's tail.

"Come on, Pig," said Goose. "Try!"

"I *am* trying!" said Pig. "But look at it! It's just useless!"

"Oh dear," said Goose, and she waddled off to the other animals.

"I think I may be able to help him," said Lamb, when he heard what had happened, and he bounced over to Pig's sty.

"Hi, Pig," he said, cheerily. "Bit of a problem with your tail, I hear."

"Does the whole world know about my tail?" asked Pig crossly. "It's fine for you, with your lovely woolly one that swings from side to side when you walk."

"But that's just the point," Lamb told him. "It's not the tail. It's the way you walk. Look, I'll show you."

Lamb showed Pig what to do.

"Just copy me, and your tail will swing, without you even trying," said Lamb.

Pig took a few steps and swayed his bottom as far as he could. But his tail stayed tightly coiled. It didn't swing. It didn't even twitch.

"Look!" wailed Pig. **"It's useless!"**

"Oh dear," bleated Lamb and off he skipped.

"Leave this to me," neighed Horse and he trotted across to where Pig was.

"Having a bit of trouble, I hear," he said.

"Trouble?" said Pig. "What would you know about trouble? You, with your smooth, swishing tail. You don't know the meaning of the word."

"Oh, but I do," said Horse. "It's *all* about trouble, you know."

Pig stared at him, puzzled.

"If you want a tail as sleek as mine, you have to take the trouble to brush it," he neighed, as he fetched a brush from his stable. "You must do it often. It won't work if you don't bother."

He began to brush Pig's tail. With each stroke, he pulled the tail straight and, at the end of each stroke, it pinged back into its old curly-wurly shape.

He brushed harder and harder.
"STOP!" yelled Pig.

"It's totally, **completely,**

absolutely

useless!"

Pig slumped down in his sty, feeling sorry for himself. He laid his chin on his feet and started to cry.

"Oh dear," said Horse. "I haven't helped very much, have I?"

"What's the point in having a tail if it's useless?" sobbed Pig.

The animals all marched over
to Pig's sty.

"Ahem!" said Horse. "We want
you to know that you have just won
the competition for the best
tail on the farm," he told Pig.

Pig stood up.

"Why?" he asked. "I can't flick it.
It doesn't waggle. It won't swing and it's
not sleek or straight. It's a...

useless tail!

How could it possibly be the best tail on
the farm?"

"Look," said Cow. "My tail can flick, but it can't curl like yours."

"My tail can wag," said Goose, "but it can't curl like yours."

"And my tail can swing," said Lamb, "but it can't curl like yours."

"My tail can swish," said Horse, "but it can't curl like yours."

All the animals tried to curl their tails – but no-one could do it.

"And that is why," they all said together, "your tail is the best tail. Because it's the

curliest tail on the farm!"

And, for the first time that day, Pig smiled.

Bright

Sparks

Thank you for buying this Bright Sparks book.

We donate one book to less fortunate children for every two sold.
We have already donated over 150,000 books.

We want to help the world to read.

This is a Bright Sparks book.
First published in 2002.
Bright Sparks,
Queen Street House, 4 Queen Street,
BATH BA1 1HE, UK
Copyright © Parragon 2001

Written by Jillian Harker
Illustrated by Simon Abbott

Printed in China.
ISBN 1-84250-535-1